# GRUDGE MATCH

Adapted by Marc Cerasini

Based on the series created by

Mark McCorkle & Bob Schooley

WITHDRAWN

New York

# CHAPTER 1

# The Gang's All Here

**K**im Possible raced down the dark street. A crazed mob was at her heels. "Pain! Pain! Pain! Pain!" the young men chanted.

"They're getting closer, K.P.!" cried Kim's best friend, Ron Stoppable.

*Yeah*, thought Kim, tell me something I *don't* know! "This way!" she called. Ron nodded and followed her down a narrow alley.

Garbage cans and trash were everywhere.

Kim wrinkled her nose as she ran. *So* not a good smell, she thought. But maybe now they'd beat that annoying mob.

As they ran, Ron looked back over his shoulder. Ron's pet Rufus, his head sticking out of Ron's pocket, looked worried. The naked mole rat was always nervous when Ron ran *one* way while looking *another*.

Just then, Rufus spotted a cluster of garbage cans right in front of them. "Whahoo! Look out!" warned Ron's little pet. Too late! *Crash!* Ron hit the cans and sent them scattering.

"Ron, over here!" Kim called from the

shadows. He crouched down beside her, next to a parked car. "I think we lost them," Kim whispered.

Ron exhaled, finally able to relax. Suddenly, a ferocious-looking dog reared up inside the car. *Ruff! Ruff! Ruff!*

"Ahhh! Teeth and slobber!" shrieked Ron.

Kim and Ron took off, but didn't get far before bright headlights shined into their eyes. A car raced out of the darkness and screeched to a halt in front of them. Three big guys hopped out chanting, "Steel! Steel! Steel! Steel!"

*Another* mob? Kim thought. Tough sitch! "Come on!" she cried, and they raced the other way. When they reached a large metal door, Ron sighed with relief. This was it— finally! They'd reached the back entrance of their destination.

Ron tried the door, but it was locked. He glanced at his watch. Time was almost up. They *had* to get inside!

The building's front entrance wasn't an option. More chanting mobs of young men had completely swamped it.

"We'll never make it!" Ron moaned.

But Kim refused to give up. "There's gotta be another way in," she declared.

"Pain! Pain! Pain! Pain!" the first mob chanted as they tramped down one end of the alley toward Kim and Ron.

"Steel! Steel! Steel! Steel!" shouted the second mob as they marched toward them from the other end.

The yells soon merged into a single chant. "Pain! Steel! Pain! Steel! Pain! Steel!"

The two mobs were both headed toward the back entrance—and Kim, Ron, and Rufus were stuck in the middle!

*So* not the place to be, Kim thought. Reaching into her pack, she drew out her portable hair dryer, which also doubled as a grappling hook.

Kim pointed the device upward and pulled the trigger. The hook shot into the air, dragging a long length of rope behind it. *Clink!* It attached itself to the roof of the building above.

Kim grabbed Ron with one arm and

clutched the grappling device with the other. "Going up," she said as the rope retracted, lifting them to the roof.

Below them, the two mobs had now surrounded the entire building. Trying to gain entrance, they pounded on the doors.

"Pain! Steel! Pain! Steel! Pain! Steel!" they chanted.

"C'mon, Kim, we've gotta get inside!" Ron said as they landed on the roof. But as he turned, Ron tripped and tumbled off the ledge!

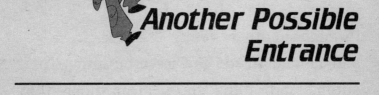

# CHAPTER 2

# Another Possible Entrance

---

**S**till clutching the grappling device, Kim dove over the edge of the building.

"Yahhh!" shrieked Ron as he fell.

"Ohhh," wailed Rufus.

But before they hit the ground, Kim reached out with her free hand and grabbed Ron. A split second later the device's rope stopped their fall.

But now Kim, Ron, and Rufus were swinging toward a brick wall. Ron thought they'd be smashed to bits. But at the last second, Kim kicked her legs out and they smashed through the building's air vent.

They tumbled down a long air shaft, burst through another vent, and landed inside the large building. After sliding across the shiny clean floor, they came to a stop against a decorative water fountain.

Hundreds of people were strolling calmly around the fountain. Not one of them had noticed Kim's and Ron's dramatic entrance. In fact, all of the people looked dazed and distracted.

Was this a secret lab filled with zombie-creating experiments? *No.* Was it an alien invasion of zoned-out pod people? *No way.* This was the Middleton Mall. And Kim was totally used to seeing people here marching around in a shopping trance.

No big, she thought. Jumping to her feet, she brushed herself off. "Next time we come to the mall, let's stick to the main entrance, okay?" she told Ron.

But Ron was barely listening. He was too busy grinning at a colorful banner: WELCOME TO MIDDLETON MALL'S WRESTLING WRIOT. Outside, mobs of wrestling fans were still trying to push their way through the choked entrances. With Kim's help, Ron had already beaten the crowd inside!

Of course, Kim was a little tweaked that she'd had to surf an air shaft to do it. She glanced down at the dirty adventure gear she was wearing. "You know, I usually like to go home and change after a mission," she complained to Ron.

"No time for that, K.P.," he said.

"Okay. *Why*?" Kim asked.

11

Ron pointed to the center of the mall, at a giant stage surrounded by cheering fans. "Steel! Pain! Steel! Pain! Steel! Pain!" chanted the audience of young men.

"The first hundred fans not to be trampled get a free GWA Tour T-shirt!" Ron exclaimed.

"GWA?" said Kim. Then she spied the GLOBAL WRESTLING ASSOCIATION banner over the stage. Another sign behind the podium read: WRESTLING WRIOT.

"How can you *not* know the Global Wrestling Association?" asked Ron. "It's only the most excellent sporting organization in the world."

Kim rolled her eyes while Ron joined in the cheering. "Steel Toe rules! Yeah!" he yelled.

"Pain! Pain! Pain!" a bunch of fans chanted right back.

Kim shook her head. "All this just because some wrestlers are making a mall appearance?" she said.

"Not just *some*," Ron pointed out. "Pain King and Steel Toe."

Kim really didn't want to hear any more. But she *so* knew she would.

"Pain King's got a bionic eye," Ron went on. "Don't even think about looking into it, or you'll writhe on the floor in total pain!"

"And I suppose Steel Toe actually has steel toes?" Kim asked.

"Nah, that's just a publicity gimmick," Ron replied. "They're more like titanium, actually. A freak industrial accident."

"Yeah!" squeaked Rufus.

Kim crossed her arms and shook her head. "Right," she said doubtfully.

Just then, an amplified voice boomed through the mall. "Listen up, Middleton! Are you ready for action?"

Wild cheers rose from the packed crowd. Kim turned to see a very short man in a silk suit standing behind the podium.

"Are you ready for head-bumping, chest-thumping, back-breaking, ground-shaking, con-fron-ta-tion?!?" yelled the short man.

"Yeah, baby!" the crowd shouted back.

Kim jerked her thumb toward the man on stage. "Is that Pain Guy?" she asked.

"No way!" Ron said. "That's Jackie Oaks, founder of the GWA."

"Now, here's a little secret," said Jackie Oaks in a loud voice. "These two world-class athletes that I'm about to bring out hate each other's guts!"

Cheers and wild applause broke out as Pain King entered. He was massively muscled and wore a blue wrestling suit and mask, topped by a golden crown.

"Pain! Pain! Pain! Pain!" chanted Pain King's fans.

From the other side of the stage came Steel Toe, his titanium foot clanging with every step. Steel Toe sported green trunks and even more muscles than Pain King.

"Steel! Steel! Steel! Steel!" chanted Steel Toe's admirers. The cheers and shouts continued until they merged into a single chant. "Steel! Pain! Steel! Pain! Steel! Pain! Steel! Pain!"

The two wrestlers met in the center of the

stage. Immediately they began pushing and shoving each other.

"Okay, I'm in the mall, and I'm *not* shopping," Kim griped. "What's wrong with *this* picture?"

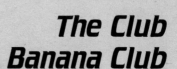

# CHAPTER 3

# The Club Banana Club

**K**im had seen enough of the wrestling stage show. She was about to leave when Ron stopped her.

"Wait, wait, wait!" he insisted. "Wrestling is more than two guys beating on each other. It's also a war of words."

Ron pointed to the stage as Steel Toe and Pain King flexed their pecs and glared at one another.

"You're going *down*!" Pain King declared.

18

"No, *you're* going down!" bellowed Steel Toe.

"No, *you're* going down!" barked Pain King.

"No, *you're* going down!" Steel Toe shot back.

Kim rolled her eyes. "Yeah," she said, "they're poets."

"Look," she told Ron. "Club Banana's doing a tie-in with the museum's Cleopatra's Closet exhibit. That's where I'll be."

Kim snaked her way through the mob and headed for her favorite boutique. Outside

Club Banana, Kim smiled at the colorful signs advertising the boutique's new line of ancient-Egyptian-inspired styles.

After pushing through the boutique's

doors, she took a deep breath of Club Banana air—the crisp scent of new clothes and price tags. She raced for a table full of trendy cargo pants, pressed her cheek against the perfectly folded pile and sighed. "Hello, civilization," she said.

"Oh, my gosh," cried a cool-looking salesperson, approaching Kim. "How much do you love Cleo's Cargos?"

"Way much," Kim replied. She smiled at the girl who was already wearing a pair of the hot new cargos.

Kim began flipping through the pile of

pants looking for the perfect pair. The sales-person whipped out a green pair from the bottom of another stack.

"You'd look good in Giza green," Kim and the salesperson said at the very same time.

"Jinx!" they both cried next.

Kim laughed. "You owe me a soda!" she told her new friend.

Meanwhile, outside Club Banana, the atmosphere was far less friendly. In the courtyard of the Middleton Mall, the "Wrestling Wriot" was getting even more riotous.

"It makes me sick to look at you, lead

foot," bellowed a chest-thumping Pain King.

"You will be so much sicker when I stomp you with cold, hard steel!" yelled Steel Toe.

Suddenly Pain King lunged at Steel Toe, and the two began to fight.

"Let's go!" Pain King cried. "Right here! Right now!"

As the two massive wrestlers grappled on center stage, Jackie Oaks jumped between them. The two athletes towered over the short promoter.

"Now, now boys," Jackie said, trying to separate the wrestlers. "Save it for *Mayhem in Middleton*." Then he winked and added,

"Good seats still available, folks!"

But the two wrestlers would not quit. Finally, Pain King shoved Steel Toe so hard he nearly fell.

"You're going down!" roared Pain King.

Steel Toe charged his opponent, slamming his head into Pain King's belly. Pain King howled in, well, *pain*.

Suddenly, the chaos on stage spread to the fans. Admirers of Steel Toe started butting heads with fans from Pain King's camp. Then they started wrestling in the aisles!

Ron Stoppable tried to escape. But as he

pushed through the crowd, a Pain King fan grabbed him and forced him into a headlock.

"Awwww!" squawked Ron. Then the crazed fan grabbed Ron's ankles and swung him around in a wide circle.

Inside Club Banana, Kim was oblivious to the chaos. She was too busy at the checkout counter, buying her new Cleo Cargos.

"Do you belong to our Club Banana Club?" the salesperson asked.

"Charter member," Kim replied, handing over her club card.

The salesperson looked at the card and

did a double take. "Kim Possible?" she cried. "I thought it was you. The stuff you do is so amazing."

Kim blushed. "Ah, it's no big, but thanks."

"I'm Monique," the salesperson replied, shaking Kim's hand. "Just moved here."

"Cool," said Kim. "Where do you go to school?"

"Middleton High," said Monique.

Kim grinned. "Me too!"

"I start Monday," Monique said.

A new best friend, for sure! "You totally have to let me show you around," Kim insisted.

"Deal!" said Monique as they shook hands.

Suddenly, Ron Stoppable's terrified scream echoed through Club Banana from outside the store. "Kim!" he howled.

Kim grabbed her stuff and bolted. "See you at school," she cried to Monique. Then she raced through the mall to—*once again*—rescue Ron.

# CHAPTER 4

# Wrestling with a Problem

**W**hat *is* this? Kim thought as she entered the mall's courtyard.

Wrestling insanity had broken out both onstage and off. Young men were flailing all over the place, imitating their favorite wrestler's moves. Above the shouts and flying bodies, Kim could hear Ron's screams.

"S'cuse me! Pardon me!" Kim cried as she leaped over a tangle of guys tussling on the ground.

27

As Kim hurried through the crowd, two men rose up to block her path. Without even slowing down, Kim leaped onto their shoulders. The guys tried to grab her, but she gracefully slipped out of reach. Then she flipped to the center of the mob, grabbed Ron, and launched herself smoothly onto the stage.

Kim's actions were so graceful and amazing that everyone stopped fighting for a moment just to stare up at her.

Even promoter Jackie Oaks was impressed. He pushed Steel Toe and Pain King aside. Then he rushed across the stage to corner Kim.

"Oh, honey, that was some performance," Jackie Oaks gushed. "You ever think about a career in professional wrestling?"

"*So* not," Kim replied.

Jackie Oaks frowned. He reached into his suit and drew out two tickets, which he thrust into Kim's hand. "I'll tell you what," he said. "Here's two passes to *Mayhem in Middleton*. Enjoy yourself on Jackie." Then he showed them the offstage exit.

Ron stared in awe at the tickets. "These are backstage passes!" he cried. "You get to go *backstage* with backstage passes! Where the *backstage* is!"

"And hang out with some guy named Steel Cage?" Kim asked in a *so*-not-interested tone.

"Uh, K.P., Steel *Toe* is a guy," Ron explained,

trying to be patient. "Steel *Cage* is, well . . . a cage."

"You take 'em," Kim said, handing over the tickets.

"You can't just give them away!" Ron cried. "Do you know what these are worth?"

Then Ron looked down at the tickets in his hand and stopped dead in his tracks.

"Okay," he said, "you *can* give 'em to me."

But Kim had kept walking. She was already ten paces ahead.

"Hey," Ron said, catching up. "Let's go back to your house and watch wrestling so we can get psyched to watch . . . *wrestling*!"

Kim shook her head. "Not tonight. I'm going to the Cleopatra's Closet exhibit at the Middleton Art Museum. It's a special preview for Club Banana Frequent Buyers."

Ron could not believe what he was hearing. "You'd rather see some dead queen's clothes than watch *Steel Toe's Night of a Hundred Bruises* with me?" he cried.

Kim sighed. "My answer would have to be—*hello? Yeah! See ya!*"

Kim walked away, leaving Ron alone with his tickets.

"Cleopatra," scoffed Ron. "Like anybody's going to remember *her* ten years from now!"

Later that night, Kim arrived at the Middleton Art

Museum. Over the huge entranceway, a banner proclaimed SEE THE CONTENTS OF CLEOPATRA'S CLOSET.

Since the exhibit was open only to Club Banana frequent buyers, only a dozen other lucky folks were in attendance. Kim smiled when she spotted her brand-new friend.

"Monique!" Kim cried. "I should've known you'd be here."

"Exclusive preview? The queen's accessories? Girl, it is all good," Monique replied.

The girls paused to admire each other's Cleo-wear. "I love your pants," Monique exclaimed.

"And you? Very Cleo," Kim said approvingly.

Moments later, a tall woman greeted the crowd in front of a giant door.

"It's my pleasure to welcome you to this special Club Banana preview of Cleopatra's Closet," the woman announced. But when she threw open the door to start the tour, she cried, "Oh, my goodness!"

The lights in the exhibit were off. On the floor lay a museum security guard, tied up with a gag over his mouth. From the darkness, beyond the door, came the sound of breaking glass.

A burglar was looting Cleopatra's Closet!

# CHAPTER 5

# To Catch a Thief

**K**im quickly pushed the rest of the crowd back. "Call security and stay together!" she cried.

Then Kim reached into her green Cleo Cargo pocket and pulled out her Kimmunicator.

"Wade!" she called. "Trouble at the Middleton Museum. Can you tap the security cam?"

"Tapping," Wade replied. Wade was the

34

ten-year-old computer genius who often helped Kim and Ron save the world!

Then Kim heard another crash in the exhibit room. There was no time to wait for Wade! Kim raced through the gloomy museum until she noticed a small dark figure enter a stairwell at the back.

Kim tailed the burglar up the stairs and onto the museum's roof. But by the time she got there, the burglar had vanished.

Suddenly, a brilliant flash nearly blinded her. It came from behind a big air-conditioning unit.

"You are *so* busted!" Kim declared as she charged forward. There was another flash of light, and she heard a doglike bark. A shadowy figure jumped out from behind the air conditioner and ran across the roof.

Whoa, thought Kim, what *is* that thing? From the neck down, it looked like a normal man, but instead of a head, the fleeing figure had big ears and a doglike snout. And he was glowing!

Guess that explains the bark, thought Kim,

taking off. She chased the figure to the edge of the roof.

Got you now! Kim thought—until the burglar leaped right off, sailing an impossible distance. The burglar easily landed on a roof across a wide, busy street.

Nobody in the world could have made that jump—nobody *human*, that is.

Across town, Kim's twin brothers, Tim and Jim Possible, were sitting in their living room with Ron Stoppable and Rufus. They all were watching GWA's *Chaos in Chicago* on a big-screen TV.

"Whoo-hoo! Toes of steel!" yelled Ron.

"Ooo! Pain King's down!" cried Tim.

"Duh, Pain

King never beats Steel Toe," declared Jim.

Suddenly, Kim burst into the room. "Ron!" she cried. "You won't believe what happened tonight."

"Shhh!" hissed Tim, Jim, and Ron, their eyes glued to the screen.

"Come on now, man!" bellowed the Pain King. "Let's see what you got!"

"You're going down!" Steel Toe replied.

Kim rolled her eyes as she waited for a commercial break.

*Beep-Beep. Beep-Beep!* Kim's Kimmunicator chirped. "What's the sitch, Wade?" she asked.

"Shhh!" Ron, Jim, and Tim hissed again.

"Sorry, Wade," Kim whispered, stepping away from the TV. "Go ahead."

"The only thing stolen from the museum was a small talisman," Wade informed her. "It was a gift to Cleopatra from the high priest of Anubis, the jackal-headed Egyptian deity of mummification."

On screen, Wade showed Kim the golden half-moon–shaped amulet. It hung on a golden chain.

"A mummy?" said Kim. "Gross. I bet she would've rather had nice earrings."

"Don't be too sure," said Wade. "This talisman was supposedly enchanted."

"Oh, come on," Kim scoffed. "Who would believe that?"

"Maybe that glowing guy on the roof?" Wade suggested.

"Good point," said Kim. "What's it supposed to do?"

"Superhuman strength," Wade said ominously.

"Great," Kim said with a sigh. "Well, at least it's not immortality, I guess," she added. "Thanks, Wade."

When *Chaos in Chicago* broke for a commercial, Ron finally walked over to Kim.

"So, how were the queen's clothes?" he asked.

"I barely got to see them," Kim replied. "Right after I hooked up with Monique, the museum was robbed by some glowing, animal-headed guy!"

"That's nice," said Ron as if he wasn't paying attention. Then the words sunk in and Ron blinked in surprise.

"Wait a minute!" cried Ron. "Who's *Monique*?"

# CHAPTER 6

# Jealous Much?

**K**im was puzzled. Ron seemed more interested in Monique than he was in a robber with a dog's head!

"Monique's a new friend," Kim said. "Really great. Anyway, the thief stole an ancient, enchanted talisman!"

"Whoa, whoa, whoa! Back up," insisted Ron. "How can I not know about a new friend?"

"I met her at Club Banana," Kim

explained. "Then again at the museum . . .
before I *chased the glowing robber.*"

"So, what's she like?" asked Ron.

"The robber?" said Kim.

"The *friend*, Kim," Ron replied. "The *new*
friend."

"Focus!" Kim insisted. "There's a glowing
guy running around Middleton with some
kind of supernatural powers."

"Okay, okay," said Ron. "Why don't we hit
Bueno Nacho and you can fill me in?"

"No, thanks," Kim replied. "Monique and
I stopped for smoothies on the way home."

Ron blinked in shock. "Smoothies?"

An hour later, Ron was sitting in a booth at Bueno Nacho. His only company was Rufus. Both of them missed Kim.

"Since when does Kim drink smoothies?" he asked his faithful pet.

Rufus jumped into a plate of grande nacho chips. "Smoothies!" he squealed, then drowned his sorrows in cheesy nachos.

"Seeing a pattern here, Rufus," Ron said. "Kim does her thing. I do my thing, and pretty soon, we're doing *different* things."

Rufus looked up from the plate. "Uh-oh," the mole rat yelped, wiping cheese off his chin with his paws.

"Maybe I'm just blowing this whole Monique thing out of proportion," said Ron. "I'll bet tomorrow everything's back to normal."

But the next morning, when Ron dropped by Kim's house, he discovered things weren't back to normal. Not even close.

"Good morning, Dr. Possible," he said when Kim's mom answered the door. "Is Kim ready for school?"

"You missed her, Ron," Kim's mom replied. "I think she said something about meeting Monique."

Ron's face fell. "Monique?" he choked. Rufus shook his head sadly.

"Oh!" exclaimed Kim's mom, "and I'm going to be late for my cranial bypass. Say 'hi' to your folks."

Kim's mom dashed off, leaving Ron standing on the front porch.

But Ron didn't stay there for long. A plan formed in his brain. To save a friend he'd make a friend. Yeah, he thought, time to fight a new friendship with . . . a new friendship.

At lunch that day, Ron put his Friendship Plan into action. When he saw Kim and Monique chatting in the school cafeteria, he walked over to join them.

"And then once, I was saving this desert prince from some stupid death squad and the back of my skirt was totally caught in my underwear. *The whole time*!"

Kim was telling Monique between bites of fruit cup.

"No way!" Monique cried as she ate her yogurt.

"I could have died,"

said Kim, waving her spoon. "He almost did!"

Suddenly, a bag of fresh, warm doughnuts dropped on the table in front of Kim. She looked up—into the smiling face of Ron Stoppable.

"Hello, ladies," Ron said smoothly.

"Ron! What are you doing here?" asked Kim.

"Well," said Ron as he sank into a chair. "Can't I dine with my best friend? And her new friend . . ."

Ron stared pointedly at Monique, and Kim made the introductions. "Uh, Ron . . .

Monique. And vice versa," she said awkwardly.

Ron reached into the bag and made a pastry offering to Monique. "Bear claw?" he asked.

"No, thanks," Monique replied. "I'm a vegetarian."

Ron stared at the pastry.

"Uh," he said, "I'm pretty sure it's *imitation* bear."

"She's *joking*, Ron," said Kim.

Ron blinked. It took him a moment to

catch up. "Good one, good one," he finally said with a forced laugh. "So . . . did Kim tell you *I'm* her sidekick? 'Cause that role's *definitely* taken . . . by *me*."

"Right," Monique said. "Well, you know, I'd better get to class. Later, Kim. Um . . . nice meeting you, Ron."

"Likewise, I'm sure," Ron replied.

When Monique was gone, Kim turned to Ron. "What is your problem?" she demanded. "You're acting really weird."

"Well, let's see," said Ron. "You went to the museum with Monique. Not me.

Monique was with you this morning. Not me. Hmmmm . . . pattern?"

"I'm not excluding you," said Kim. "It's just that you and Monique are . . . different."

"Oh, now you're going to tell me that sometimes growing up means growing apart. I've heard it before, Kim." Ron paused to wipe away a tear. "Billy Bawlwiki, second grade."

"You are so blowing this out of proportion," Kim said.

"Okay, maybe I am," Ron sighed. "Oooo, don't forget . . ." Ron whipped out the wrestling tickets, ". . . *Mayhem in Middleton*!

Tonight."

"Those tickets are for you," Kim replied. "I kind of already made plans with . . . uh . . . Monique."

There was dead

silence for a moment. Then Ron frowned. "I blame the smoothies," he said.

He leaped to his feet and tossed the tickets on the table. "Here," he said. "Jackie gave these to you."

"And I gave them to *you*," Kim replied.

"And I'm giving 'em back to *you*!" Ron cried. Then he snatched one of the tickets back. "Except this one," he added. "But only because it'll be the highlight of my life."

Then he turned and walked away.

"Ron!" Kim cried. But he was already gone.

# CHAPTER 7

# Mayhem in Middleton

**O**utside the local arena, wrestling fans were lining up at the gates. They couldn't wait for *Mayhem in Middleton* to start!

Backstage, Pain King and Steel Toe were in their dressing room, preparing for the big event.

"So," said Pain King in a slightly bored tone. "Are you taking a vacation this year?"

"Yeah, we went ahead and rented a cottage out on Martha's Vineyard," Steel Toe

replied. "You know, it will be nice to get a chance to relax with the wife and kids."

Pain King nodded. "Sounds charming."

Just then, someone knocked at the door. The two wrestlers jumped to their feet and angrily waved their fists at one another.

"I hate your guts!" shouted Pain King.

"I'm taking you down, slime," barked Steel Toe.

The door opened and in walked Jackie Oaks.

Pain King relaxed. "Oh, Jackie, phew," he said.

"Man," said Steel Toe. "I thought you were a reporter or something!"

"Hey, listen," Jackie said. "What do you guys think about me getting into the ring

with you tonight, huh?" He stood as tall as he could.

Steel Toe and Pain King looked down at the promoter—and chuckled.

"C'mon, Jackie. Be reasonable," said Pain King.

"Yeah," Steel Toe added. "I don't mean to sell you short—oops—"

Jackie glared. "Very funny, very funny, yeah," he snapped.

"Sorry, man, I didn't mean it like that," said Steel Toe sincerely.

Pain King patted Jackie Oaks on the back.

"Stick to promoting, Jackie," he said. "That's what you're good at."

Jackie frowned and left the dressing room. Out in the hall, he reached into his pocket and pulled out a golden chain with something hanging from it shaped like a half-moon. It was Cleopatra's enchanted talisman!

"Ah," said Jackie with an evil grin. "This is all going to change. . . . Tonight!"

Meanwhile, near center stage, Ron Stoppable waved at two big guys sitting in the front row.

"Hey! Nice seats!" Ron called.

"Yeah, definitely!" one of the guys boasted.

Then Ron waved his own ticket under their noses. "But not as nice as mine!" he boasted right back. "*Backstage,* baby!"

Ron and Rufus slapped a high five as they reached the stage curtain.

"Gonna see my man, Steel Toe," said Ron as he flashed his pass to the bored security guard.

The guard grunted and pulled the curtain aside.

Ron and Rufus wandered backstage, taking in all the sights, sounds, and smells of Global World Wrestling—up close and personal.

Ron spotted Pain King and his hero, Steel Toe.

"It's Steel Toe! And Pain King!" he squealed. "So close I could touch them! But I won't," he decided. "Because I'm *cool*."

"Yo, Steel Toe. 'Sup, Pain?" he said.

Then Ron just couldn't help himself. He reached out and patted Steel Toe on the back. Even Rufus put his little paw out.

"I touched Steel Toe!" Ron cried.

"Whoa, me too!" squeaked Rufus.

Steel Toe stared at Rufus and frowned. "Your gerbil's totally bald, man," he said.

Ron was giddy. His wrestling hero had actually *talked* to him. "Yes! Thank you!" he cried. Then Ron totally lost it. Forget cool, he thought. I want to remember this moment forever! He pulled up his shirt and exposed his belly. "Could I have an autograph?" he asked. "Could you make it to, um, to Ron?"

"Uh, sure. Let me get a pen," said Pain King. He turned and yelled for his promoter. "Yo, Jackie!"

"Yeah," said Steel Toe, looking around. "Where is that guy? I need my sunglasses, pronto."

"I'll get them!" Ron offered. "Can I? Please? Please? Please?"

Steel Toe nodded. "Sure, kid. They're in my dressing room."

Ron rushed to the dressing room. Little did he know that in that very room, a strange ritual was underway.

Candles burned all around. The smell of incense filled the room. In the center of the space stood Jackie Oaks. But instead of his usual silk suit, Jackie wore Egyptian garb and sandals. Around his neck hung the talisman of Cleopatra.

"All right, let me see if I've got everything," Jackie mumbled as he studied his *To Do* list. "Open-toed sandals, check. Talisman—oh, it's glowing. That is nice, uh, beautiful, yeah."

Then Jackie took from his costume another list. This one was older—much, *much* older. It was written on a piece of cracked and yellowed parchment.

"My ancient papyrus," Jackie continued,

"which I shall now read from—*Anubis, protector of the tomb, your time is now the time of doom.*"

As he chanted the magic words, an eerie wind blew through the dressing room.

Then Jackie's eyes began to glow. His muscles bulged. His teeth became fangs. His ears grew into points and his nose lengthened into a long snout. He was transformed into an eight-foot giant with a jackal head!

He stood at the open door, his mouth gaping. The *thing* that was Jackie Oaks turned to face Ron, teeth bared in a bestial snarl.

"You know what?" Ron whimpered. "I can come back later." Instantly, the jackal-headed creature snatched him up. With a savage roar, the monster threw Ron out of the dressing room.

Ron flew through the air and struck a food-service cart. Sandwiches flew everywhere. A quivering Rufus jumped out of Ron's pocket and hid under a piece of lettuce.

"You want to be left alone. I'm down with that," Ron told the creature.

Still growing, the jackal-headed giant burst out of the dressing room, roared once again, and shook its mighty fists at the ceiling.

"Tonight," it roared, "the world will see the fearsome power of . . . the Jackal!"

# CHAPTER 8

# Just Call Me Jackal

The Jackal, now ten feet tall and still growing, grabbed Ron in one mammoth paw.

"I've seen!" Ron howled. "I believe!"

Laughing evilly, the Jackal hurled Ron down the hall and through the curtains. Yelling, Ron sailed over the crowded arena and slammed right into Steel Toe, just as he was about to grapple with Pain King.

Steel Toe went down. The crowd jumped to its feet and booed Ron.

Pain King grabbed Ron by the shoulders and shook him. "What are you doing?" he cried.

Ron pointed to the opposite end of the ring. "Uh, there's a problem," he said weakly. "Him!"

Pain King stared in disbelief as the glowing, ten-foot-tall figure of the Jackal stepped over the ropes and into the ring.

Meanwhile, far away from the mayhem, Kim was sitting with Monique at Middleton's most popular coffeehouse.

Monique was in a good mood, but she could see that Kim wasn't. "Not enough froth in your latte?" Monique asked.

"No," Kim sighed. "I'm just feeling guilty. I kind of blew off Ron to be here tonight."

"Why didn't you bring him along?" Monique asked.

"Unless someone put a waiter in a

headlock, this is definitely *not* Ron's scene," she said. "Besides, he had a date with Steel Toe."

"He scored tickets to *Mayhem in Middleton*?" Monique exclaimed. "The GWA rocks!"

"What?" cried Kim.

"Pretty tacky, I know," Monique confessed. "But my brother hooked me up. Pain King's my boy."

Kim slapped her forehead. "I can't believe you and Ron have something in common."

Just then the Kimmunicator chirped. Kim whipped it out of her pocket. "What up, Wade?" she asked.

"More on that talisman," Wade replied. "If the holder recites an incantation from an ancient text, the spirit of Anubis could actually possess him."

"Sounds bad," said Kim.

"Very," Wade assured her.

"So, we'd better find that ancient text," Kim noted.

"Too late," said Wade. "Somebody already found it. Some masked guy stole it from the university in Chicago."

Kim nodded. "Do you have access to the police report?"

Wade tapped some keys and the report appeared on the Kimmunicator screen.

"The thief was supershort!" said Wade. "And the GWA was in Chicago before Middleton!"

That clinched it! Kim

had to go before it was too late. She jumped up and grabbed her backpack.

"Sorry, Monique," Kim said. "I keep running out on you."

At Middleton Arena, the Jackal stood in the center of the ring.

"Who is this guy?" Pain King asked.

"Man, beats me," said Steel Toe.

"It's Jackie," Ron told them. "He's got supernatural powers!"

"Jackie Oaks?" said a surprised Pain King.

"You all said I was too small to get in the ring!" roared the Jackal. "Well, here I am! You still think I'm too small?"

Then the Jackal reached out and grabbed a wrestler in each gigantic paw—and the crowd went wild!

"The Jackal's awesome!" the guys in the front row cried.

Boldly, Ron walked right up to the Jackal

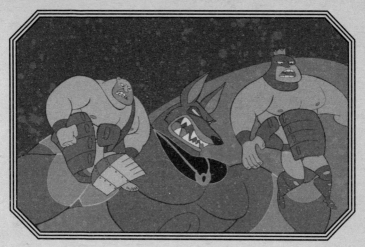

and commanded, "You made your point, Jackie. Now put them down!"

"I am no longer Jackie!" the creature roared. "I am now . . . the Jackal!"

Then the monster fired glowing bolts of power from its eyes. The beams struck Ron and sent him flying across the ring and into the ropes.

Yikes! Takedown!

# CHAPTER 9

# *Tag-Team Time*

**K**im Possible dashed into the arena and forced her way through the mob. "Excuse me. Pardon me. . . . Excuse me, I'm gonna squeeze through here," she said politely. Finally, Kim decided she had no time for manners.

"Out of my way!" she yelled. The crowd parted and Kim rushed to the ring in time to see Ron break down completely.

"First, I lose my best friend, now

professional wrestling! Everything's ruined," Ron sobbed.

"You didn't lose your best friend," said Kim.

"K.P.?" said Ron.

"And don't worry," said a determined Kim Possible. "We're going to save this . . . this . . . uh . . . Would you call it a *sport*?"

Ron jumped to his feet. "The most excellent one ever," he declared.

"Ron, are you okay?" Kim asked.

"Kim!" Ron cried, a new realization hitting him. "You decided to use your ticket!"

"I think Jackie is the museum thief," Kim told Ron.

"Old news," Ron replied. "The question is, what now?"

Kim jumped over the ropes and into the ring. "Let's take him down!" she declared.

Ron and Kim gave each other a high five.

"I'd tag team with you any day, K.P.!" said Ron.

"This'll be easy," said Kim. She believed it, too. Until she saw the Jackal twirl Pain King and Steel Toe like a pair of batons!

The Jackal released the wrestlers and they flew into the ropes, bouncing off and slamming into one another in the center of the ring.

"I will take on all comers in a no-holds-barred grudge match. Right here! Right now!" the Jackal declared.

The Jackal gazed out at the crowd. Then he fired twin bolts of fire from his eyes.

"Awesome rocket effects, bro!" shouted a fan.

"Prepare to be body-slammered, Jackal," said Kim.

"That's body-*slammed*," Ron said. "Better let me do it."

Ron grabbed the Jackal's leg, but the creature kicked him away. Ron landed on the ropes with a thud.

"You go," Ron told Kim.

Kim looked up at the Jackal. "Why don't you try it *without* the talisman?" she taunted.

"Why don't you make me?" roared the Jackal. With a wave of his hand, he made Kim float up into the air. "I am all-powerful," he declared. Then he let Kim drop to the mat.

"Ouch!" said Kim.

As Ron rushed to help her, Kim's eyes narrowed on the jackal-headed jerk. "You distract him. I'll go for the talisman," she told Ron.

Ron gave her a thumbs-up. "Distraction. Solid!" he cried.

Ron strode boldly up to the creature.

"Steel Toe's number one!" Ron yelled. "Jackal who? Jackal who? Steel Toe's number one!"

The Jackal spun on Ron.

"That's right, you heard me, old demon," said Ron.

As the Jackal stalked forward, Kim climbed the ropes behind the creature. With a leap she landed right on the Jackal's back. Kim reached over his shoulder and grabbed for the talisman. But the Jackal snatched Kim off his back and hurled her toward the ropes.

"Whaa!" cried Kim.

"From now on, the world will bow down to *me!*" roared the Jackal. Then he leaped over the ropes and into the panicked crowd. Fans scattered as the Jackal smashed seats and threw them aside.

Kim jumped to her feet. "As long as he has that talisman on, this guy can't be stopped,"

she said. "Ron, you keep the Jackal busy."

"I did that already!" Ron cried. "And I have the rope burns to show for it."

"Doesn't have to be for long," said Kim. She pointed to Pain King and Steel Toe. "Get them to help."

Ron ran up to the wrestlers. "We've got to keep the Jackal busy!" he cried.

But the wrestlers shook their heads. "No way, man!" Pain King replied. "The guy is scary."

"There's no way," said Steel Toe. "I don't want a piece of this guy. His eyes are glowing."

"Gentlemen," said Ron. "You are not just

73

entertainers. You are not just gifted athletes. You're heroes!"

Steel Toe and Pain King exchanged glances, then smiled. Ron was right. "Let's get it on!" the wrestlers cried together. Then they challenged the Jackal. With a roar, the creature turned toward Steel Toe and Pain King and leaped back into the ring to face them.

Above them on a catwalk, Kim smiled. With the Jackal back in the ring, she quickly attached her grappling hook to the catwalk. Then she grabbed the cable and swung over the side!

As the Jackal knocked the two wrestlers around, Kim swung by him and tried to grab the talisman. She got a nasty surprise when beams from the Jackal's glowing eyes cut the cable in two. Down she plunged!

Kim spun in the air and bounced on the wrestling ring's ropes. She flew over the Jackal's head to the other side of the ring—but she couldn't grab the talisman!

Ron pulled Rufus out of his pocket and aimed the mole rat at the Jackal.

"One chance, buddy!" Ron cried. Then he hurled Rufus through the air!

"Noooo!" bellowed the Jackal as Rufus snatched the talisman from his thick neck and continued flying past.

"Gotcha, Rufus!" Kim cried when she caught the flying mole rat.

A wind blew through the arena, whirling around the Jackal, who suddenly shrank in size. The Jackal head disappeared. A moment later, Jackie Oaks stood in the center of the ring, staring up at a very angry Pain King and Steel Toe.

"Um, ha, ha, guys," whined Jackie. "Be reasonable."

But Pain King snatched Jackie up and twirled the helpless promoter over his head.

"Jackie, you're going down!" Pain King cried. Then he hurled Jackie into the audience.

Kim, Ron, Rufus, and the wrestlers waved as the crowd went wild! "Dude, that's the best, most awesome, most totally rippin' show I've ever seen," cried one fan.

"No way, man!" yelled another fan. "The whole Jackal thing was totally fake!"

# CHAPTER 10

# The More the Merrier

The next day, Kim, Ron, and Monique sat in a booth at Bueno Nacho. Each had a plate of burritos in front of them.

"You know," said Monique. "I still can't believe you met Pain King and Steel Toe."

"I can't believe you're into wrestling," said Ron.

Kim rolled her eyes. "I can't believe I know either of you," she groaned.

"Enough talk!" Monique cried, lifting her

burrito. Then she challenged Ron to an eat-
ing contest. "In the immortal words of Pain
King, *you're going down*!" said Monique.

"*Au contraire*," Ron replied. "It is you
who will be going down."

Ron and Monique stared at each other,
burritos at the ready.

"First one to drip is the loser," Monique
declared.

"Better get your bib, baby," Ron laughed.

"So wrong!" cried Monique.

Rufus hopped onto the table and raised a
napkin to signal the start of the contest.

"Ha ha, go!" squealed the mole rat, dropping the napkin.

As Ron and Monique began gobbling up their burritos, Kim looked on in disbelief. Then she shrugged. "I think this is the beginning of a very weird friendship," she said with a laugh.